NICKELODEON

Rugrats in Paris
THE MOVIE

JOKE BOOK

K L a S K Y
C S U P O INC.

Based on the TV series *Rugrats*® created by Arlene Klasky, Gábor Csupo,
and Paul Germain as seen on Nickelodeon®

SIMON SPOTLIGHT
An imprint of Simon & Schuster Children's Publishing Division
1230 Avenue of the Americas, New York, New York 10020

Copyright © 2000 Paramount Pictures and Viacom International Inc.
All rights reserved. NICKELODEON, *Rugrats*, and all related titles, logos,
and characters are trademarks of Viacom International Inc.

SIMON SPOTLIGHT and colophon are registered trademarks of Simon & Schuster.

Manufactured in the United States of America

6 8 10 9 7

ISBN 0-689-83197-8

RUGRATS in Paris
THE MOVIE

JOKE BOOK

by David Lewman

Simon Spotlight / Nickelodeon

New York   London   Toronto   Sydney   Singapore

Stu: Knock, knock.
Didi: Who's there?
Stu: Francis.
Didi: Francis who?
Stu: France is a great country—let's go!

Why did the bugs go to Paris?

They wanted to be
French flies!

**What does
Dil use to
hold his
pacifier?**

His Binky finger.

What happened when the pig visited the Bobfather?

His wish was grunted.

Why did Chas go over to the palm trees?

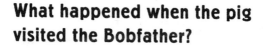

He was looking for a date.

Tommy: When do ducks get married?

Susie: On their webbing day!

Why did the bride and groom get married in a fountain?

They wanted to have a beautiful wetting.

Why did Lou tease Lulu?

He wanted to kid the bride.

Lou: Why did the bride and groom spend hours in the garden?

Lulu: It was their weeding day!

Phil: What song do ducks play when they get married?

Lil: "The Wedding Marsh."

Tommy: What did the chicken wear to the wedding?

Chuckie: A *clucks*-edo!

Why did Angelica climb on a faucet when the music started?

She wanted to tap-dance.

Why did the couple hold their reception at a playground?

They wanted to swing-dance.

What do you call two salamanders who just got married?

Newtlyweds.

Lil: Knock, knock.
Phil: Who's there?
Lil: Paris.
Phil: Paris who?
Lil: Pair us up—we're twins!

Why does Didi give Dil so many vegetables?

Every time he wants something, he says "peas."

What do you call two spiders who just got married?

Newlywebs.

Why did Angelica ride a bike down the wedding aisle?

She heard flower girls are supposed to have pedals.

What does Tommy's new grandma sing to him at night?

Lulu-bies.

When is Chuckie like a bell?

When he's a ring bearer.

Why did Phil want to go to Grandpa Lou's wedding?

He wanted to see him throw the gardener.

What's it called when Tommy dances?

A baby
boogie.

Why can't babies get married?

They don't know how to
tie the knot.

Why did Phil eat lots of grapes before he went to see the Bobfather?

He'd heard that he was supposed to be very grapeful when he saw the Bobfather.

Why do bears get married?

Because they love going on honeymoons.

Why did Angelica want to bring scissors to the wedding reception?

Grandpa had said they were going to cut a rug.

Why did the groom look at his bride's watch?

He wanted to have the time of his wife.

Why did the two pieces of meat get married?

They fell deeply in loaf.

What do you call someone who loves Ms. LaBouche?

A Coco-nut.

Why did Reptar get mad at the rehearsal for his show?

He kept losing his head.

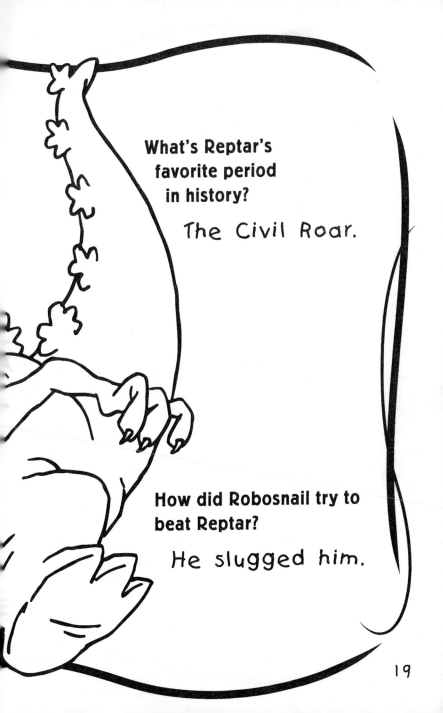

What's Reptar's favorite period in history?

The Civil Roar.

How did Robosnail try to beat Reptar?

He slugged him.

19

What does a chef pack before a trip?

Her soup case.

What does a snob pack before a trip?

His snoot case.

Lil: Why was the butter grouchy?

Phil: It got up on the wrong side of the bread.

Where do rabbits go to catch a plane?

The *hareport*.

Where do ghosts shop in Paris?

At the BOO-tiques.

Lil: What happened to the ball that got squished?

Phil: It's no longer around.

What does Robosnail pack before a trip?

His *sluggage*.

Why did Lil cover her eyes with her hands when she was in front of the clothing store?

She was playing peek-a-boutique.

When Coco was a girl, what was her favorite part of school?

Show-and-yell.

Coco: Knock, knock.
Kira: Who's there?
Coco: Queen.
Kira: Queen who?
Coco: Queen up this mess, the princess is coming!

Why is Coco always angry?

Because she's a MADemoiselle.

Chas: Knock, knock.
Howard: Who's there?
Chas: Gargoyle.
Howard: Gargoyle who?
Chas: Gargoyle after meals for fresh breath!

Why did the pig write "marry me" in the mud?

He wanted to plop the question.

What's Coco's favorite color?

YELL-ow.

What does a giant use to eat soup?

A bowlcano.

Chas: Knock, knock.
Drew: Who's there?
Chas: Eiffel.
Drew: Eiffel who?
Chas: Eiffel awful,
let's get off
this tower.

Why is Dil always throwing balls down?

He already knows how to throw up.

How often does Robosnail fight Reptar?

All the slime.

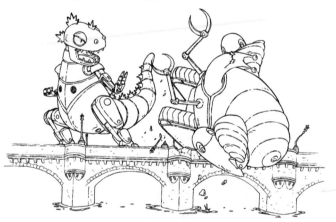

Why did the referee pull the ball out of the game?

It was out of bounce.

Where does Chas keep his inhaler?

In his breathe-case.

Did Chas find his razor before the wedding?

Yes, in the nick of time!

When did Tommy know they had followed Kimi into a cave?

Right off the bat.

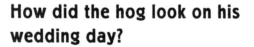

How did the hog look on his wedding day?

Very hamsome.

Where do skunks sit in church?

In the pee-yews.

How did Quasimodo know it was Coco's wedding day?

He just had a hunch.

What did Angelica say after tying Jean-Claude's shoelaces together?

"Have a nice trip!"

How do you keep a wedding ceremony from breaking up?

Tape the whole thing.

Why is Coco so bad at growing plants?

Because she has a mean thumb.

What happened when Reptar tore off the top of the souvenir shop?

Prices went through the roof.

Chas: What do you get when you cross Chuckie's stuffed bear with a cantaloupe?

Didi: A Wawa melon.

Why did the ball want to keep going down the hill?

It was on a roll.

What kind of tea does Coco drink?

Nas-ty.

How is Angelica's cat like a cloud?

She's white and Fluffy.

What lives in the desert, has fangs, and weighs three hundred pounds?

A sumo rattler.

Angelica:
Why did the piece of bread go to Paris on the hottest day of the year?

Susie: 'Cause it wanted to be French toast!

33

Howard: What do kings do when they have visitors?

Betty: They put out the welcome moat.

Lil: What did the water say to the castle?

Phil: "Pleased to moat you."

Charlotte: Which part of a castle is the most artistic?

Drew: The *drawbridge.*

Tommy: Which painting do cows like best?

Angelica: The Mooooona Lisa.

Angelica: Which painting do ghosts like best?

Susie: The Groan-a Lisa.

What does Chas eat when his allergies are bad?

Sneeze and crackers.

Chuckie: What's Spike's favorite painting?

Tommy: The Bone-a Lisa.

What was Spike's favorite thing to see in Paris?

The Arf-ful Tower.

What was his second favorite thing?

The Bark de Triomphe.

Stu: What do you call a French dog who loves America?

Grandpa Lou: A Yankee poodle.

Phil: Why did Chuckie cover his hair with a book?

Lil: He wanted to be a read head.

Drew: What did the chicken say to the chef?

Stu: "Whenever you're in town, cook me up."

Phil: What kind of key opens Dil's mouth?

Lil: A Binky.

Howard: At Lou's wedding, how was the punch?

Betty: Oh, it was a big hit!

Susie: What do chickens do before a trip?

Angelica: They peck a bag.

Why was the duck late for his flight?

He spent too much time quacking.

Chuckie: Why did Dil hang around Spike's neck?

Tommy: He wanted to play tag.

Charlotte: Does Dil like it when you let him yell?

Didi: Yes, it's a scream come true.

Betty: Why did Stu and Drew sleep all the way to France?

Didi: They wanted to have a pillow flight.

Lil: Why did the airplane marry the jet?

Susie: It was love at first flight.

Tommy: Why are you afraid of getting stung in the hotel?

Chuckie: I heard hotels have lob-bees.

Why was the potato sad at the Princess Parade?

He got a lump in his float.

Betty: What happens when babies really like each other?

Didi: They crawl in love.

Angelica: What do you get when you cross candy with an alligator?

Phil: Crocolates.

Angelica: In that cold warehouse, did you talk with your teeth or your tongue?

Susie: My teeth—they did all the chattering.

What's Dil's favorite ride?

The stroller coaster.

Why don't parades ever sink?

Because they're full of floats.

Phil: Where do cows go for fun?

Lil: The a-*moo*-sement park.

What's Spike's favorite ride?

The rover coaster.

Angelica: Where do pigs go for fun?

Susie: The amusement pork.

Tommy: Knock, knock.
Chuckie: Who's there?
Tommy: Spark.
Chuckie: Spark who?
Tommy: 'S park is fun!

Why wouldn't Charlotte take Angelica on the ride?

The whine was too long.

What do tourists use to get around the beach?

Taxi crabs.

Who brings you dessert on a plane?

The pie-lot.

Where do Phil and Lil get their worms back after a flight?

The *bug*-gage claim area.

Why did the artist sketch everyone waiting for the ride?

He had to draw the line.

What gives big hugs and goes great on toast?

Momalade!